This Book belongs to

....

Princess Pistachio
and the Pest

Marie-Louise Gay

Translated by Jacob Homel

pajamapress

First published in the United States in 2015

Text and illustrations copyright © 2015 Marie-Louise Gay
This edition copyright © 2015 Pajama Press Inc.
Translated from French by Jacob Homel

10 9 8 7 6 5 4 3 2 1

The publisher gratefully acknowledges the support of the Canada Council for the Arts and the Ontario Arts Council for its publishing program. We acknowledge the financial support of the Government of Canada through the Canada Book Fund (CBF) for our publishing activities.

Library and Archives Canada Cataloguing in Publication

Gay, Marie-Louise, [Malheurs de princesse Pistache. English]   Princess Pistachio and the pest / Marie-Louise Gay.
Translation of: Les malheurs de princesse Pistache. Translated from the French by Jacob Homel. ISBN 978-1-927485-73-6 (bound)
       I. Homel, Jacob, 1987-, translator II. Title. III. Title: Malheurs de princesse Pistache. English
PS8563.A868M3513 2015   jC843'.54   C2014-906881-6

Publisher Cataloging-in-Publication Data (U.S.)

Gay, Marie-Louise, 1952-
    Princess Pistachio and the pest / Marie-Louise Gay.
Originally published in French by Dominique et Compagnie: Saint-Lambert, Québec, 1997.
[48] pages : color illustrations ; cm.
Summary: Forced to abandon exciting plans with her friends and take baby Penny to the park, Pistachio is sure her first day of summer holidays will be boring. But keeping Penny out of trouble proves to be more exciting than Pistachio expected.
ISBN-13: 978-1-927485-73-6
1. Humorous stories. 2. Sisters – Juvenile fiction. I. Title.
[E] dc23   PZ7.G39Pr 2015

Cover and book design–Rebecca Buchanan

Manufactured by Qualibre Inc./Print Plus
Printed in China

Pajama Press Inc.
181 Carlaw Ave. Suite 207 Toronto, Ontario Canada, M4M 2S1

Distributed in Canada by UTP Distribution
5201 Dufferin Street Toronto, Ontario Canada, M3H 5T8

Distributed in the U.S. by Ingram Publisher Services
1 Ingram Blvd. La Vergne, TN 37086, USA

We acknowledge the support of the Government of Canada through the National Translation Program for Book Publishing, an initiative of the Roadmap for Canada's Official Languages 2013–2018: Education, Immigration, Communities, for our translation activities.

To my friend Lucie Papineau

· Chapter 1 ·
A Bad Start
to Summer Vacation

"Pistachio Shoelace!" Mrs. Trumpethead shouts. "Are you listening to me?"

Pistachio is startled. Mrs. Trumpethead's face looms over her. Her eyes shoot lightning. Her eyebrows are small, slimy black vipers.

"Y-y-yes, Mrs. T-t-Trumpethead," Pistachio stutters.

"Then answer my question!" Her teacher hollers.

Her black vipers gather at her brow in a V.

"What is two plus two?"

Total silence. You could have heard a tadpole diving. A fly flying. Pistachio, desperate, thinks as hard as she can.

"Um…," she mutters.

A few children start laughing.

"Two plus two?" Mrs. Trumpethead roars.

"Five?" mumbles Pistachio.

Half the class bursts into laughter.

"Six?" she whispers.

The entire class is rolling on the floor.

"TWO PLUS TWO!" bellows Mrs. Trumpethead.

Her black vipers wriggle and squirm. Her nostrils flare. A real dragon.

"Four! Four! Four!" Pistachio screams, but her teacher cannot hear her.

Pistachio wakes up, screaming, in her bed. The dog is gently licking her cheek. Sunlight floods her room.

"Phew!" she breathes out. "What a nightmare!"

And just then, Pistachio remembers that it is the start of summer vacation!

"Hurray!" she shouts, jumping out of bed. "Hurray! No more school! No more mean old Trumpethead! No more homework! Time for adventures and freedom! Hurray!"

Pistachio throws her clothes on. No
crown for her this morning. She slaps
on her baseball cap, takes her backpack
and her flashlight, and careens down the
stairs. She rushes into the kitchen like
a tornado. She's singing loud enough
to rattle the windows. Loud enough to
wake the neighbors.

"No more pencils, no more books, no
more teachers'—"

"My princess…," her mother stops her.

Her voice is too soft. Her maple
syrup tone. Pistachio looks up at her
mother with suspicion. But her mother is
smiling at her. A smile that would melt a
snowman in winter.

"My princess," she says again,
"could you take your sister to the park
this morning? I've got work to finish.
Please?"

Pistachio's heart falls to her belly button.

"No way!" she says. "It is the first day of summer vacation—and I am supposed to meet up with Madeline and Chichi—we're going to explore the cavern down at the cemetery—and then—"

"Pistachio," her mother says, "I need your help."

There is no more maple syrup in that voice.

"No fair!" Pistachio protests. "I am going to die of boredom with her—"

Her mother is no longer smiling. A cold gust of wind blows through the kitchen.

"I go park!" Penny shouts, "With Pish-tasho!"

"Oh, no," Pistachio sighs, discouraged.

"Oh, yes!" her mother says. "I am sure you are going to have all sorts of fun. Right, Penny?"

Penny's smile reaches both her earlobes. She has squashed banana in her hair, on her nose, and even in her ears.

"Eeeeew!" Pistachio says.

· Chapter 2 ·
A Little Thief

Half an hour later, Pistachio hits the road. She is dragging behind her the wagon piled high with dolls, stuffed animals, plastic buckets, shovels, rakes, and…her little sister! Penny wears her rabbit-ear hat and her Superman cape. She looks ecstatic. She has also managed to hide the dog under a stuffed elephant.

"Did you have to bring every single toy you own?" Pistachio grumbles, out of breath. "I feel like a work horse."

"Gee up, Pish-tasho! Gallop, gallop, Pish-tasho!"

And here come Madeline and Chichi on their bicycles. When they see Pistachio, they brake, their tires screeching. The wagon disappears in a cloud of dust.

"Hey, Pistachio!" Madeline says, "Are you coming with us to explore the cavern down at the cemetery? We have candles and a compass."

"No," Pistachio mutters. "I have to take my sister to the park."

"What?" Chichi sneers. "You prefer playing dolly with a baby?"

Madeline and Chichi zoom off, laughing like monkeys.

"But…but…," Pistachio begins.

Too late though. They are already far away.

"Rats! It's not fair! My friends get to have great adventures, and I have to spend all my time with a baby."

"I not baby! I Super-Rabbit!" Penny shouts.

"Yeah, right, sure…," Pistachio mutters, rolling her eyes. "I Tarzan, you Super-Rabbit!"

Under a burning sun, Pistachio walks slowly. Behind her, perched on the mountain of toys, Penny sings, "Giddy up, Giddy up, Giddy up up up!" at the top of her voice.

The dog is snoring. Pistachio is daydreaming about exploring the cemetery's cavern. It is dark and silent. Suddenly, a rustling, a whisper: bats are brushing past her with their humid wings. She almost jumps out of her skin when she hears a growling voice coming from behind her.

"Stop! You! Stop right there, you little thief!" shouts Mr. Pomodoro, the local grocer.

He is as red as a tomato. He looks furious.

"Are you not ashamed! What a bad example for your *piccola* sister!"

"What? What's going on?" Pistachio replies, flabbergasted.

A small crowd appears around them. People are whispering and pointing fingers at her!

"And what's-a-more, you pretend to be innocent! *Mamma mia!*" Mr. Pomodoro says.

He digs his two arms in the pyramid of toys and dolls. He wakes up the dog, who, surprised, begins to bark.

"And this, what is this?" the grocer asks, brandishing two bananas.

Pistachio's eyes go as wide as saucers.

"And this? This is a beach ball, maybe?"

He puts a melon under her nose. The crowd laughs. The dog barks even louder.

"But, but… where does it all come from?" Pistachio asks, a bit dazed by the brouhaha.

"From my stand! *Mamma Mia!* If I ever I catch you again, you little good-for-nothing, I'll call the *polizia!*"

On that note, he turns and walks toward his shop, head held high. The crowd disperses, muttering.

"What a disgrace!" The baker says. "But who is the little thief?"

"Pistachio Shoelace!" Abraham replies, sneering. "She is in my class."

"Ah! Kids these days!" sighs an old man. "When I was young, these sorts of things never happened!"

Pistachio stands there, like a statue, her mouth open and her cheeks burning red. She does not understand any of it. Then she sees her sister sneak a pear from underneath the stuffed goat. She takes a big bite from it.

Pistachio finally understands. Penny is the thief! She is the little good-for-nothing, not Pistachio! Anger rises in her like a strong wind, hot and red. She grabs the pear out of her sister's hands and hurls it into the street. *SPLAT!* A car squashes it like a pancake.

Penny howls, furious.

Pistachio's eyes are stormy black and her teeth are clenched. She sets off for the park again, pulling behind her a sulking rabbit, its ears flapping sadly. The dog follows them from far behind, his tongue hanging like a pink sock.

• Chapter 3 •
Oldtooth the Witch

Pistachio finally sees the park's entrance at the end of the deserted street. All of a sudden she spies her friend Rachid rollerblading toward her, bent under the weight of his large backpack.

"Ho! Pistachio! Are you coming to explore the cavern at the cemetery? I hear there is an amazing treasure right down at the bottom. I have a pickaxe and a shovel. Madeline and Chichi are bringing—"

"—Candles and a compass. I know, I know," Pistachio sighs, "but I can't go. I have to—"

"Take your dolls for a walk?" Rachid interrupts, laughing.

"I am bringing my sister and HER dolls to the park, can't you see?"

"Your invisible sister, I am guessing?" Rachid adds.

"My sister is invis…?"

Pistachio turns around. The dolls and stuffed animals are looking back at her with a stunned air. But where is Penny?

"Have fun, Pistachio!" Rachid calls out, then he vanishes in the blink of an eye.

Pistachio, in a panic, looks from one
end of the street to the other. Empty!

"Find Penny!" she tells the dog.

The dog turns around, nose to the
ground, ears flapping in the wind.
Pistachio follows him closely. Suddenly
the animal stops in front of a stone wall,
one leg in the air.

"Pish-tasho! Pish-tasho!" A squeaky
voice calls out.

It is Penny, perched all the way up on
top of the wall, like a bird on a wire.

27

"Don't move!" Pistachio says.

"I Super-Rabbit," Penny shouts. "I fly!"

She swirls her cape and prepares to jump into the air.

"NOOOOOOOOO!" Pistachio howls.

Penny, surprised, falls…on the other side of the wall. Pistachio hears a soft cry. Then, total silence.

Panicked, Pistachio climbs the wall. The old mossy stones are slippery. She breaks her nails and scratches her knees. Pistachio carefully peeks over the wall and sees Penny lying flat on her stomach in a sea of red flowers. She is as still as a mouse.

Oh, no! Pistachio thinks. She jumps down into the garden and runs to her little sister.

"Penny?" she whispers.

No answer. Maybe her sister is seriously wounded? Maybe she is dead? Pistachio is afraid. Suddenly, Penny jumps up and bellows, "Surprise! I Super-Rabbit!"

She bursts into laughter and falls back into the flowers. Red petals swirl in the air.

Pistachio is both very relieved and very angry.

"You bird brain!" She shouts. "Wait until I—"

"What are you doing in my garden?"
A loud, creaky voice complains. "You
little pesky pests. You have come to cause
trouble, I know!"

Pistachio turns with horror to see Mrs.
Oldtooth approaching them, holding
herself up with her bent cane. Small, fat,
and hunchbacked, she hides her nasty
old face under a large black felt hat.
All of the neighborhood kids know her.
Everyone calls her Oldtooth the Witch.

"I would not mind turning you both into toads," Mrs. Oldtooth grumbles.

"I hungwy!" Penny shouts.

Her rabbit ears waggle over the flowers.

"Hush!" Pistachio says between clenched teeth, "do not be scared!"

"I not scawed!" Penny shouts. "I hungwy!"

"I am hungry as well," Mrs. Oldtooth growls, "I would not mind chomping on a bit of plump rabbit. Yum-yum!"

She hobbles closer, one hand digging in her huge hairy handbag.

"Yes, yes, a nice rabbit stew. That would not be bad at all. With a warm toad soup—oh, just delicious! Well, now! Where did I put my magic wand?"

Mrs. Oldtooth puts her handbag on the ground and sticks her whole head into it, searching for her wand.

"You little pests," she says, her voice muffled, "just you wait and see!"

Pistachio takes advantage of
Oldtooth's distraction. She grabs Penny
and carries her under her arm like
a small sack of potatoes. She starts
running toward the wall.

"You will never get me, you old
witch!" Pistachio hollers.

And just like that, she climbs over the
wall and disappears on the other side.

Mrs. Oldtooth takes her head out of
her bag and looks up. She smiles.

"Works every time," she says.

Her creaky laugh echoes in the empty
street.

• Chapter 4 •
Pistachio's Treasure

Finally, they are at the park. Pistachio sets Penny down in the sandbox with her bucket, her shovels, and her stuffed animals. Pistachio collapses on a bench under the shadow of a tree and wipes her forehead. *Whew! That was close!* she thinks.

As she is catching her breath, she starts daydreaming again of the cavern in the cemetery.

If only she could explore it… She would be the one to find the hidden treasure. She is sure of it! She sees herself crawling in a narrow and humid tunnel, a candle in her hand. All of a sudden, she sees a glowing light. No, two! The eyes of the dragon, guardian of the treasure. He is lying on a pile of gemstones, jewels, and gold coins. The dragon opens his smoking maw wide and howls—

"Pish-tasho! Pish-taaaa-sho!"

Pistachio jumps up. She turns around and sees Penny swimming in the fountain's basin. Suddenly her sister dives, splashing all the pigeons. SPLASH! You can only see her stripy socks. She reappears immediately, a big smile on her face.

"Pish-tasho!" she shouts. "Come see!"

Pistachio is furious. What a pest! She runs to the fountain.

"Penny! That's enough! Get out of there right now!"

"I found a tweasure!" Penny shouts.

A treasure? Pistachio comes nearer. Penny places a handful of coins on the side of the fountain. She smiles proudly.

Pistachio clenches her jaw and tells her sister, "You fish head! That is not a treasure. People throw coins in the basin to make a wish. It is forbidden to take them out."

"That is exactly right!" a serious voice says.

It is the park warden.

"It is also prohibited to swim in the fountain, prohibited to walk on the grass, prohibited to bring animals without a leash," he continues.

"Those are stuffed animals!" Pistachio protests.

From the corner of her eye, she sees that the dog is hiding behind a tree.

The man takes a small black book
from his pocket and reads out loud.

"Article 213, paragraph b): *It is strictly
prohibited to bring any animal (stuffed or
alive) without a leash to the park.* There!"
He says, satisfied. "Now, get out of my
park. Miss, you should be ashamed of
yourself, forcing this sweet little girl to dive
into the fountain to find money for you."

"But, but…," Pistachio stammers.

"No buts! Get out!"

The warden places his black book in his pocket and crosses his arms. Pistachio grabs her dripping sister, who is flopping about like a fish, and places her back in the wagon.

She leaves, head down, under the furious stare of the park warden. Penny, all smiles, waves at him. The dog follows them like a shadow, hiding behind tree after tree.

The two sisters finally get back home around noon. Pistachio, red and breathless, pulls behind her a very damp and wrinkled Super-Rabbit.

"So?" Their mother asks. "Did you have fun?"

"Pheeew!" Pistachio sighs. "Thanks to Penny, I was accused of theft, then I was almost turned into a toad, and, worst of all, we were kicked out of the park. I am done! I am not going to take care of this brainless baby anymore."

"Not baby," Penny shouts, "I Super-Rabbit!"

"What amazing adventures!" her mother says. "I have the impression that you were not bored for a second, my princess, right?"

Pistachio stares at her mother. *On what planet does she live?* she thinks. *She doesn't understand anything!*

"But on the other hand, maybe it is too much for you. Tomorrow, I will ask a neighbor to come and keep an eye on you both."

"Who?" asks Pistachio, curious.

"You know her: dear, sweet Mrs. Oldtooth."

"Oh, no!" the two sisters shout in unison.

Pistachio immediately says, "Don't worry, Mom. I will take care of Penny tomorrow. I am sure we will have fun. Right, Penny?"

"Yes!" cries Penny. "You Tarzan, me Suuuuper-Rabbit!"

44